Stretcher Bearer

Jeanell Buckley

Stretcher Bearer

Stretcher Bearer
ISBN 978 1 76041 491 7
Copyright © text Jeanell Buckley 2018
Cover: *main photo* – stretcher bearers from bottom of trench, by
Ernest Brooks – this is photograph Q 1332 from the collections of
the Imperial War Museums (collection no. 1900–09), Public Domain,
https://commons.wikimedia.org/w/index.php?curid=569373; *book
of tags* – by http://wellcomeimages.org/indexplus/obf_images/
e3/bd/bd755119307108347d2d7c25fe98.jpgGallery: http://
wellcomeimages.org/indexplus/image/L0058806.html, CC BY 4.0,
https://commons.wikimedia.org/w/index.php?curid=36212530

First published 2018 by
GINNINDERRA PRESS
PO Box 3461 Port Adelaide 5015
www.ginninderrapress.com.au

Contents

Giles

1

April 1916

Private Giles XXXXXX, Xth Div.
Australian Medical Corps
Maadi Camp, Egypt

Dear Molly

It was all so rushed that day in Sydney when the ship was being loaded, we never got to say a word of goodbye or good luck or any of that sop. Sweat was pouring from me after that march from Moore Park and, boy, don't the crowds know how to pinch and grab? A handful of limp daisies is no substitute for a moment of quiet. We're heading off to war. Don't they understand what a burden that puts upon a man's mind?

So why did you not stay and wave me off?

The corporal at the embarkation office had said you could come aboard, as your ship was embarking pretty soon after. 'So your sister's in the service too, eh?' He had a wad of paper as long as my arm, a spike through the lot and the wind fluttering in them like flags on Empire day. 'Women more trouble than they're worth in a war – still, trained nurses, brave girls all of them. Older than you?'

'Twins. And very close.'

'Ah, you'll make your old Ma proud.'

He scribbled with that thick pencil and, by golly, did my stomach take a tumble, for he could have checked it, sure enough. You were gone by then, so all a waste, and me lying about our ages to the army for nothing. And if I shudder at a white lie, what will I be like with a Hun in front of me with a bayonet aimed at my guts? Have you seen anything of this modern weaponry?

Before I forget, I actually missed seeing you this side of the world by only three hours! The minute I got your note saying you were in Alexandria en route to France, I ran to the sergeant to get leave but my train broke down on the way, and I got to the wharf only to hear that your ship had left. If only we'd hitched up, together we could have hired a driver and gone out to the pyramids. Incredible, isn't it, that they're over 10,000 years old? Maybe old Moses passed them on his way out into the Land of Israel?

It's now three months since I padded along those dusty farmers' roads and landed in Liverpool camp. You were there with the cloth flag, and those woollen socks you gave me then are still with me – too hot here, but in the Old Country, well… Now you're nursing, you'll have no more time for knitting. Are you treating Australian men in France? I hear the Tommy hospitals are run like barracks, with the wounded forced to sit up and salute and the Aussie girls talking back to officers good and proper. Dearest Mol, I can only imagine how well you obey orders – I don't think so!

Maadi camp is a mighty establishment. I have piquet duty with the colonel twice weekly, mess duty at breakfast, as well as the fatigue and trench work. The sand is a bugger – it flows back into the trenches as soon as you give it the shovel. You'd think with all this invention for war, the machine guns and the motor lorries roaring around, they'd come to a better system for making trenches. The horses would be no good and anyway, what place is this for horses? The Gypos and their camel trains know the drill – you never see them off on sick parade. But the Gypo can't fight this war without the white man, to be sure, so perhaps between the two of us we can beat Fritz.

So far I've received five letters here – yours, two from Mother, one from Lionel and one from Angus in Dubbo. Angus wants to join up but Uncle Tim thinks he should complete his bookkeeping course. He's only six months off, and Angus thinks the show might be over by then, and maybe he's right. I only just missed the big push at Anzac Cove. What a day it must have been. I dare say a missing arm or leg will be nothing back in Australia when the victory's won. What's a chap to expect otherwise in war?

I don't know when you'll get this, Mol. The mail is a bit irregular at present. The chap I share this tent with hasn't had one letter.

'Maybe yours is in the sea now, mate?' the mail private had suggested to him. A Tommy destroyer had gone down taking sweethearts' notes and tinned puddings with it.

'Na,' he answered, rolling his tobacco. 'They've all forgotten me. The lot of them, bastards.'

He made me glad I have any letters at all.

There's a queer unnatural feel to the desert. The shivers at night with only one blanket, then the scorchers in those trenches. It's similar in the bush, Mol, I know. Angus tells me right enough. But home there's the sound of the cicadas, the galahs and the bats. Here in Maadi there's just the unwelcome scorpion in the tent, the whistles when the guard changes, a few drunkards arguing with the natives – baksheesh, baksheesh – and the spitting camels. I'd love to talk to you about it, Mol. But I can't. Not at this distance.

If you get this, please reply to my regimental address. It may be slow, but the letter will find me somewhere. Just don't mention places in any of these foreign lands for, as you probably know, the censors will destroy any letter which reveals too much to Fritz. This may be the last letter I can post independently. Few men going on leave are brave enough to carry another man's mail out for him or, even more risky, his photographs. My experiments with a camera will have to wait until I return to Sydney.

Regarding your question about the transfer, I can't agree with you. Yes, your pals in the corps will miss you, but London has plenty of work for Aussie girls. There are even lady tram conductors and bus drivers there and if the nursing becomes too much you can change while still doing your bit. Besides, Mother worries about you, and she's not the only one.

Your brother, Giles

2

Dear Mother

We arrived at Maadi camp at 16.30. I must get used to this 24-hour clock (military style, and much in use on the European continent, we've been told). Maadi is not much of a place but we've been told that from now on there's to be no mucking up with the locals. Cairo was too crowded for me anyway, Mother. The mess in the streets has to be seen to be believed. The household debris is thrown from the upper storeys and no shouts of 'watch out below' are issued to the random passer-by – not that any of the boys know the local tongue anyway, except the words we need to buy from the fruit seller boys – baksheesh (which means 'money') and so on.

I miss the horses – this is no land for them. There were some real beauties in the officers' stables – a pale mare which I was told was descended from Scarlett Heart, two black colts not liking this place much but good-tempered otherwise, and a lovely little horse which was the colonel's (the colonel planned polo matches for the senior men, but the higher-ups put the cosh on that, which we all were sorry to hear). They've been moved to the canal, I hear – they were no use in this sand. A camel corps is being established and men asked to come forward, which of course I won't be, Mother – I'm not much of a horseman. I hope Molly's able to keep up her riding in the nursing corps. Do you know if they have horses? I've received one letter from Molly and one from Lionel. The old girl's grown-up now – I'm so proud of her.

I'm enjoying all the extracts from *Town and Country* and the boys are enjoying the *Bulletin* right royal. You've no idea what it means for your name to be called out when the mailbags arrive. And golly don't they arrive in droves, and usually a month behind. I just received yours dated 10 February, but I received the 3 March one before (the day before yesterday), so you see how organised the army system is – I think not!

So anyway, there's so much it's hard to know what to leave out and what to put in, as I'm usually whacked at the end of the day and the boys get lights out called at nine o'clock (21.00 hours) most nights. I sleep like a top even though the boards are hard as nails and the pillow the roughest bag of hay I've set my head upon. The work is real stuff, Mother, and I'm not complaining! But the sand and the flies can go to h—. (Pardon my language. You'd be out of your skin if you heard the boys cursing in the drill behind me!)

We get plenty of food, and it's good – mutton stew, potatoes, beans, rice custard and tea. The biscuits from the canteen are all right. The sand is the worst – it gets into your water, into the eyes of the horses, those that are here, poor beasts. No wonder they're being moved back to the stables in Seraphim.

I just missed seeing Mol by three hours, her ship landing in Alexandria for only twelve hours, and it taking me five hours to get away from Maadi and through the chaos of the train stations. I don't even think she was able to see the Old City, but then it's not fit for a white woman's steps anyway.

Passing the officers' mess while there, you won't believe who I did meet – Gavin Pye, my school chum. What a lucky break. He's in the post office with a septic leg. He was evacuated from the Dardanelles. What a time he must have had! I envy him and all those boys, the Glory of our good old Empire! What a life it seems since we were at the dances in town and just kids. Gavin is very tanned and lean. To be honest, he looks tired and older (that's what war does, I suppose).

He knocked off at seven so we went to the NCOs' mess and had tea and a biscuit, and while there a guard outside took a shot at one of the roaming dogs. Cairo is full of them, Mother. They get left behind when the Gypos take market out to the desert towns. Well, as the shot was heard, Gavin jerked down to grip the table side. His hand was sweating hard and it turned out, Mother, that he has war nerves, very common in the men from the trenches. He has to work indoors mostly, and can't be outside where he sees long and far as he fears a Turk bullet still. And the post office is good, being in some old mosk (a kind of church, Mother), as it's dark and he can pretend he's underground again.

I don't think he'd mind me saying about the nerves, as the doctors say it's part of war and not cowardice as those newsmen have been hinting. Being in the ambulance corps, I'm getting an idea of what's normal and what's not here close to the front.

Anyway, as yet, I have no nerves or fear that I won't be able to do my bit. But I do miss everyone like blazes. Mol seems to be settling into the nursing all right, but the south of France is too close to the front for my liking. She's loyal to the other corps girls – has she told you she tends some of the graves in the town where a number of nurses have been buried? Tuberculosis has struck down many of them. The workload is high and I suspect they don't take enough rest.

I must sign off now as the lights are going out and I'm still to get my kit in order. Tomorrow I start the real stuff. There's plenty of drill and everyone in the company must learn all basic duties – bayonet, duck and dive, trench drill and carry, gas drill, bandage and splinter work. But as I'm in the AMC I don't have to go full pelt in the heat running with pack as the infantry does. We have practice carry for two hours six to eight a.m., then breakfast, then two hours bandage lessons, burns clean, and gas mask fatigue (which makes all the boys crack up – it's a riot, Mother).

PS: The heat is awful, over 100 most days by noon, and the officers have worked out a better roster, so we rest from two o'clock to half-past four. Must sign off. The mail leaves at 20.00 hours tonight.

Your loving son, Giles

3

June 1916

At sea

Dear Mother

I'm writing on the deck of HMAS *XXXX*, and I'm glad to say we're saying farewell to old Egypt and the shores of Arabia. The desert of Maadi camp is now behind me. Sand has burrowed into the folds of the bags, and we shake it out and refold. I even have grains on this piece of paper! Inspection is by Sergeant Frazer and he makes sure we get the right practice in folding the kit if we've got it wrong. Sergeant Frazer was there at Anzac Cove and he's a real veteran now, twenty-five years old, and knows the ropes as far as sand and keeping clean are concerned. The ship is headed for France, we believe, but where I cannot say (I like to cheat the censor, Mother, a little joke between me and him!). Sergeant Frazer said that no Anzac should let his body get too soiled as it leads to the lice and infection which then cause disease. They used to wash in the sea at Gallipoli and no matter if Abdul shot a round into the water, the boys just kept it up. Brave if you ask me, but according to Sergeant Frazer, there wasn't much choice with the chats (that's lice) in everything, and all the fresh water for drinking. He made it out of the Dardanelles, and he doesn't say much except that he owes his life to Abdul, 'cause he took a bullet in the thigh while he was under the water. The Turk guns, being Hun-made, are efficient and long-range, and Abdul's sniper was to blame (what a way out, not even in battle, but the bath!) One poor chap had his privates blown off by such an incident and so Sergeant Frazer counts himself lucky. They got the Abdul sniper in the end, so he said, a kid no more than seventeen.

Sergeant Frazer displayed the spot, a pink rash of a thing streaking down the leg. They showed Abdul mercy – I think not!

Seasickness is rife here, Mother. I had to hold my writing paper aloft just now because a private was displaying his tea across the deck. Plenty have been laid up with it. Being in the AMC, I'm doing plenty of first aid. One broken leg yesterday when a wave hit and a chap fell down the ladder to the lower deck. The bone was near the surface. I tried to push and you should have heard the curses. No stretchers here – all the gear was left in Seraphim for the next recruits. We suppose the army manages this stuff all right. Some of the lads were greatly upset as the khaki hats and great coats have been stowed away below deck – for the return home, they said, but one chap said they were dropping them over the side. Like those newspaper rumours of bodies being taken from the Dardanelles and dumped at sea. Sounds ghoulish, doesn't it? But I don't carry with that one. (Will the censor take that bit out about the rumour? It has been in the news already, but we have no idea how strict or otherwise the censors are.)

The doctors give us plenty of lectures on board and, as I'm now in this line of work, I attend as I should (I'm sure the officers would note any absences). Last night we were told about venereal disease and they take it very seriously, as it can affect any man's fighting capacities. We're told the moral side too and, as we're men fighting a cause of Honour, the loose morals many men showed in Cairo cannot be continued. I am sorry, Mother, to describe this unpleasant side to you, but that is life here in the army!

It's not just the body, but the mind we're learning about. The doctors say the war nerves will be tested in the front line in France as well as here in the east. The Hun can be counted on to wreak havoc in the mind, and we'll be hard-pressed battling it.

I can't wait to compare notes with Mol on this. How odd that we should both land in the medical corps. I've urged her to make the move to London, for she needs lively company, and what a feather in her cap if she should land herself a Tommy officer over there! She was never one for boats, so I pray she's not posted onto a hospital ship.

4

July 1916

XXXXX, France

Dear Mother,

The journey settled down pretty well after my last letter and that night (19.00 hours) we landed at Calais, where the train met us. I can't describe the beauty of France in bloom in the summer time, the trees the greenest I've ever seen, gems glistening in the fast windows of the trains. The widows (everywhere here, Mother, the men have gone) are black spots in the fields. They bend and pull at the crops and dirt is flicked across the train windows as they call out '*Adieu* Khaki!' They love the Anzacs. They lean in when the train slows and give us strawberries and apple cider from their big jugs. Plenty of crying too, Mother. All along the line are the crosses of the dead, with women kneeling in the dirt.

Our billets are a great barn with massive beams above it like a cathedral, and so much is old here, it might as well be a cathedral. I have a chum here, a veteran of Anzac, who I shared a carriage with (the journey was three days, Mother, with plenty of stops and getting on and off). He's not nerve-wrecked like many of them. He also is an AMC and, his duties in the Dardanelles behind him, says that if he could stand that hell, he can stand anything. His name is Stan and he's got a girl's way with jewels and trinkets which he says he collected from the bodies (those that couldn't be identified).

'What's the use in the Turk ground?' he said, although I can't defend this stripping of the dead. He says we did it to the Turks good enough and this is more out of respect than anything. Stan has a Gypo chain and on it are three crucifixes, a Lady of Fatima, a St Christopher medal, and, from a Hun, an Iron Cross with a stiff red ribbon. The sergeant knows all about them.

'Good-luck charms, sir,' he said.

The sergeant laughed. He's an Imperial man who says he's seen worse thievery in the regular army.

I have time to tell you this, Mother, because I can't sleep. Stan practised a bandage on me and the bandage was full of chats, so now I'm copping it in the legs of my trousers and in my underwear. Stan has taken a pair of silk drawers from a bombed-out bedroom and wears them while he sleeps, so no chats disturb him – yes, I know, Mother, like something out of *Punch*! That's the army for you. Heaven help the wounded we're supposed to treat out at the front. The straw creeps with beetles – they come in with the crops the French store here. When the guns blow, the tremors send dirt down from the potatoes stored above us (the guns are eight miles away, but we feel it in the earth – the sky lights up like a summer storm).

I forgot to say, I received your letter of 15 June just today, and it was most distracting. We read bits aloud to each other at night by a candle – unless the Hun Taube aeroplane's coming over, which they do all night, then it's lights out and all the boys to the doorways to watch the light show. The roar of our shelling is tremendous – if it does that to the trees all twisted and shattered, great oaks and poplars across the roads, holes five feet deep and ten across in the mud – what does it do to a man? So far, I'm yet to touch a wounded man. I'm being kept in reserve, which means keeping the kits and the dressing stations in order, ready for the wounded. But so far there's nothing.

But something is going on. The roads half a mile from here are choked with horse trains and mules. The ruts must be seen to be believed. We can hear them from here trudging all night to the front.

Stan's a good man, and I think you'd like him, Mother. The captain is an odd one – he laughs for no reason. His eyes don't like me, so I hope I'm not in for a bad run.

Rain all night and then this morning the boys had a six-mile march round the villages, which is how they keep us ready for the front. As I'll be carrying, I have to be as fit as the infantry. The roads are composed of giant pebbles. It's hard on the boots and some of the horses have tumbled. A chap I met yesterday called Shilling has a job as a groom to a colonel. He's a bush man from the old Light Horse and cares for a lovely beast called Nutty. He has the firm quietude of a man accustomed to animals. Shilling's battalion has been cut up, and he's been shunted from here to there all round the front since then. Now that he's only a groom, he can't wear the smart hat they're famous for.

'Lucky to have a horse to hand at all,' he said. 'Some officers ride in motors now. There are roads in the Sinai, made special for the motor, where no horses can go.'

We were standing near a field and, Mother, it was nothing but slush to the knees. The French women pick at the edges trying to keep some crops alive, but every day another acre goes into the sky. Oh, the noise of it, the thrill of it and, oh, I know it sounds a sinful pleasure, but so it is. The sky's alive when Fritz gets his iron ration.

Shilling and I talked of the wonder of these fired nights.

'But I don't fancy the trench life,' he said. 'Men aplenty wanted my job. I was lucky to get it. My Peninsula service saw me right with the colonel.'

'You were there?' I asked. He bore no obvious signs of wounding.

'Dysentery saw me on my back for a month – a cursed thing.' He spoke warmly of lying in muck for hours while men with a bullet in the arm were treated ahead of him. His ire was rising but, thankfully, the colonel approached us and ordered Shilling to saddle the mount.

Most of our officers are fair in their own way. Our captain has a warm way with the men in great numbers (meaning he takes the drill seriously). Only today he gave a man thirty minutes more drill at day's end for being five minutes late on parade. But the men appreciate him in the line for his nerve. He's twenty-four, only a year older than me, Mother, and he's been an officer for three years, with two years of service behind him.

Please remind Mr Sutter that I'm grateful to him for keeping my place at Ingroves safe. That's one thing about this war. Men at home and enlisted, they alike know the value of it. If Fritz is to be beaten, how else but by the efforts of nations alike, all the men fulfilling their duty for Empire?

I mentioned in my last letter, Mother, Stan the chap with the strange ways. Well, he's a wag. He's making a flag to lay in his stretcher, all made from spare clothes left by the Frenchies. The village close by still has two shops, a chemist and a bar. But the shelled houses flap open to the rain and the mud splatters the hanging doors.

'What a waste,' he said last night. 'It'll all go to pot in this weather. And what if Fritz breaks through? He'll have it all, won't he?'

'What if they come back?' I asked. 'The Frenchies?'

'We're fighting to keep Fritz at arm's length from them, aren't we? We're entitled to their homes.'

'We are fighting the same war, I suppose.'

'Yes, plenty of spare rooms now with so many of the menfolk on permanent tour. I suspect some of these widows appreciate a man in the house again, if you follow.'

A shell went over then, making the timbers shudder. One poor old cow lives with us in the corner of the shed. Its udder swells some days as there's no one to milk it. Madam in black, who owns the land now her husband is deceased, she gets in when she can and whispers to the old girl. It's hard on them, with so many gone. The cemetery was bombed last week, someone told me, and what bad luck after so many just put into the earth. It took days to sort out the limbs and place them again. The wailing from the grieved women keeps the men awake. Last week an infantryman was court-martialled for mistreating a woman – he shoved her hard, not meaning to, she slipped on the icy ground and bruised her elbow, and wailed even more till the officer came. Then what a to-do ensued.

The general feeling is mixed on the subject here. The men of his company feel for him as he was thirty-six hours in Needle Trench and, marching eleven miles back to the billet, found the canteen had been hit. That was it for any hot food. It was then apparently, going back to the billet hungry, that he hears the wailing and it set him off. If only, one chap said, he'd slept on the roadside, he'd have not gone down that darkened alley where the lady resided. He'd have not heard the shrillness and, my, the Frenchies can make a racket.

Shelling again, Mother. It makes a man nervous as a cat. That's how the men look, coming from the trenches late, their streaming, gassed eyes the only pulse of light left in them.

I hear it may be tonight we go out for our first go at Fritz. I say 'we' as I'm attached to the XXX Company, Mother. I carry for them now, which is not what I expected when I left old Sydney town. It's not my body I worry about, despite the fact that the carries are miles long, and plenty of mud and slush to get through. How will it be for me out there with my nerves? It will only be then that I'll know if I'm fit to be in this war.

Your loving son, Giles

5

Dear Lionel,

This is my first chance to write for three days. What an agonising time we've had. I daren't write too much, and oh, the censors are cruel to deprive a man of this relief. I'm sure the Hun knows more than a stretcher bearer and, if not, well, they're doomed in this war.

We are resting under some sheets of iron four miles from the line. There are eight of us at present, one corporal and seven of us privates. The fellows have all been through this sort of hell before and it's a great relief to have men experienced in such horror to pull me along when it gets warm outside.

I'm in number 5 outpost. It's a mile from number 4 outpost and so on right up to the line. Tonight we've had a quiet one and it's a blessing, as I doubt my arms would lift another stretcher if I tried. It's not like training. The carries happen while the shells fall around us. The earth near this outpost is nothing but a swamp – my feet are sitting in mud as I write. Sleeping is impossible for, if the shells aren't falling, the canvas sheet that keeps the rain out flaps non-stop in my ear.

Last Tuesday (was it only two days ago?) we were ordered to set out through a half-sown field up to the front. A cow wandered here and there while its dead mate rotted some way off. The French hobble along through it all. So many are without homes now, but they will not desert their fields.

At night, the front can be seen from miles away – the bombardment is a lightning storm which flashes over the whole land. A church spire was on our left. It's a talisman to the boys of the AMC. Inside, they say, the Huns crucified kittens, one of the men from the Fusiliers swore to it. I was attached to this outpost, number 5, and supposed to be in reserve. But no sooner had I arrived than we were ordered to move up and carry.

It was as I would imagine hell to be, Lionel. A fire in the sky, and the eerie glow from the flares was not wholesome. As we reached the sap, a shell exploded and I thought I'd died. The very ground shook and liquid seemed to run from me in waves, and it was a relief. Am I a coward, Lionel? For in that moment I felt that death would surely take me, and I would thus not face that which was coming to us. I was happier to be dead than serving my King and my nation in this massive struggle.

As we approached the sap where the trenches start, a horrible shape came into view. I cannot call it a single shape, for it was really a number of them, some slithering like a bag of snakes, some stuck at angles as I've seen in carters' shops when carriage spokes are in the making. If it were not for the noise of it, I would have kept going, for the industry of war produces so many strange sights. But the cry of a man – how can that be misheard?

'What is that?' I muttered, not expecting to be heard.

'A right mess of a pillbox,' answered Cockie, my partner. He held the far end of the stretcher and kept his pace towards the sap.

'Listen, Cockie!'

'I can hear enough…' His words were nearly obliterated by shellfire. 'Come on then.' It was Cockie again. 'Just leave it!'

We had stopped momentarily and he was angry with me. His round face was bloated with the exertion of yelling. In my side vision was the horror. Cockie was not more than three feet from it but seemed not to notice it.

A swoon came over me, and an officer, who I knew had come from the sap, was yelling. He was head to toe in mud – only his face gleamed with sweat illuminated by the red of flares. I had seen him smile before but, in the moment, he seemed ready to murder me. Someone must have given me a kick along and I started forward. Maybe those weeks in Maadi on the sandy grounds had worked – I was obeying my superiors without thinking.

Then the hours of carrying. Cockie's little voice never ending, before me man after man who have blurred into one. The narrow trenches where we could barely squeeze between the men, the weight of bodies, my ears ringing from a bullet which struck my helmet, the noise of machines shifting guns and ammunition. After it all, my first taste of rum issued by the boys in the hut the following night – twenty-four hours carrying, a night and a day of Sausage Gully, one and a half miles one way to outpost number 4, then back. Six of the carries across the blackness. I had assumed the nights would be the worst. I'd heard rumours of others abandoned by drunken guides in the wasteland, the wounded man being carried in circles for hour upon lost hour. How does one compare horror to horror? Dawn brought what I could never have thought possible in a civilised world.

I'm sleepy with a second nip of rum, and the lads have tried to bury that moment for me along with the dead. It's not allowed of course – strictly speaking we're still on duty – but the sergeant has looked the other way this time for my sake.

'If them back home knew about what gets done round this place…' Cockie had cooked rice pudding over his primus stove, his fat stomach covered by a girl's apron, feeding me from a silver spoon pilfered from the ruined chateau over the hill. 'Better now?'

I didn't like that tone he used, that note of paternalism. I'm too sensitive maybe. But in our little hut the world recedes, and this becomes the world, the mingling of chlorophyll, cigarette smoke and rotting wool. The sight of the boys facing me across the tiny gloom – Cockie the mother to all of us.

'Here, look what I salvaged,' he said, bringing out a book of photographs.

Girls in stages of undress, pretty things, pale legs and breasts. The boys sighed over it, one of them fingering the flimsy pages as I've seen women finger fabrics in Mr Ingrove's shop. We were all drawn to these small squares of loveliness.

'Where did you get this, Cocky?' asked Clyde. He's a scowling man who, being a bank clerk, expected to obtain a commission, but he has landed with the AMC. The photographs even made him smile. 'Is that German there?' There were a few words in small print along the edge.

'No. From a house in the village. No secrets left in this war. See?' He then pulled forth a pocket watch with a chain which he quickly hid again, teasing us with the treasure.

My pal Stan from infantry played a similar game with his trinkets but he was sent to the front a week before me. He didn't trust the mail with his treasure and wanted me to smuggle them out with a wounded man. But I had refused.

'My father has a watch such as that,' I piped up. For some reason, I felt the need to contribute some tale of my own.

'Oh, so you've no need of more trinkets, Giles. You'll inherit your own. Lucky lad. I can see you promenading on George Street with one and a lady on your arm to match.'

They laughed at this as if it was a ridiculous thought. I've become the hapless infant in their company. There I was urging Molly to move out of harm's way as if I were the senior of us two. To think she's probably bandaging the same torn flesh that I carry on my stretcher. Through these poor wounded devils, we are, in a funny way, working side by side.

I want to sleep but do not want a return to the wretched dawn of today. There had been birds in the shredded trees, so few left and so their voices more keenly lovely. The smell of burning from a field kitchen, and I noted my lack of hunger, was proud of my stamina through the long carries of midnight, two and three, the mess between. It was my first return to the sap, and I heard English voices all round. The Welsh boys were in, the captain of last night back in his bed by now. The pillbox was still there and still a seething monstrosity. And a single feeble sound, a boy's voice, came forth from the mess – an Australian, hoarse-throated, and the sound was muffled by the clog of bodies. Then nothing, gone. I could not believe it when I heard laughter from the trench. Some excitement over a fruitcake apparently, our own Comfort Fund stores delivered to the Tommies by mistake. On days such as this it can be hard to love the Empire.

Your brother, Giles

Sidney

6

Private diary of Captain Sidney XXXX
Xth Division, AIF, Western Front

18 July 1916

The first mail for a month. A note from George about Lil's marriage, and how overdue that was. The old girl will be well set up with a wool man. He's a decent chap but his hearing kept him from enlisting. Lil feels for him, I'm sure, missing the great jaunt, but he's better off out of this mess. A pressed flower from Lil in the very next letter I open – the gold of the Hunter Valley, a strand of heaven, and I can smell the old house from here. It's in the back of the diary now. I'm getting quite a collection – the wild daisy from the trench at Lone Pine and the piece of camel hair I caught in my stirrup. The cruelty of the camel drivers, the slit nostrils and the bleating, rise from its wool, but I have the aroma of trench foot to distract me now. I should have asked that Hun prisoner we took how his side is dealing with this blight. Too many stretcher cases of it, such an unmanly affliction, and a waste of men whose hopes of glory have been disappointed. They bear up, though, except the language is warm and unworthy of soldiers fighting for the King.

We relieved two companies of Welsh Fusiliers at two a.m., the relief taking two hours longer than it should have because the officers were in chaos. Colonel Lennox, being seriously wounded, has left a large gap in their command. Too young, the captain I took briefing from was a plump-faced boy with roses in his cheeks. His handwriting in the log is real private school: 'Left flank under barrage 12–12.45. Return barrage from 1.15 after Pioneers cleared a length of trench. Forty-five men killed from Section 4, another forty wounded. They fought gallantly and will be missed.'

It's form stuff, these words. They must teach it at Sandhurst, and perhaps he needs to prepare ground for mentions later on. Many of these English lads suffer at the hands of their own men. English soldiers do not respect their officers. Plenty of saluting and woe betide a NCO who fails to salute even under a barrage. They all, men and officers, despise the b— Australians for their lack of formality but, if the scrape turns warm, they like to have us there to take the fire.

Savage rushed into the sap just before stand-to (5.30) to say the Pioneers and some of the bearers were in a stoush over a carry. The Pioneers think that as he's been wounded he belongs to the bearers, but the bearers claim the man's dead and so the ball's back with the Pioneers.

I lost my temper at Savage then. Such a shame that the weather was so glorious outside the trench. I heard a lark that very second up in the wood (or what's left of it) over on our right flank. God bless 'em, they carry on singing whether there's a bombardment on or not.

'Where's the trouble?' I asked. What do we have officers for if not to deal with such bickering?

'In the fire trench. I think the bearers just want a rest, sir.'

'Have they checked the man's pulse?'

'I don't know, sir.'

'They are medically trained, Savage.'

'The Pioneer sergeant says it's – well, that they just want out of the carry. If the chap's dead, that's one thing, but…'

If he's not, if he is indeed alive, then he's the bearers' burden, not that of the Pioneers. There's little a man won't do to get out of what he proudly embraced as his duty only a month earlier. I keep my distance from the bearers – they're a callous band. Their hardness as they tramp about the fields, scurrying along the duckboards and around the filth, hunched like vultures – it's an odd bravery which must be paired with coldness in order to bear fruit.

'Go and find out, Savage, then report back.'

I dragged some maps across the table then, flicking flies from the papers with my cap. A mile back then for Savage, knee-deep through water in the communication trench, then returning. By the time he made it, the chap would be dead, no doubt, then I'd hear it from the Pioneers that a whole body was the job of the Sappers. Why didn't someone just shove the poor chap up onto the parapet with the rest of them? The flies were on my neck. If my lieutenants did their job, the corpses wouldn't stay more than a day or two. But the bodies do the job of the sandbags we should have received weeks ago, and the men would give the officers no thanks for removing another yard of cover.

A quiet stand-to. I think Fritz was shoring up two miles of trench in the north and I couldn't blame him for trying to sort it out. Our sap was flooded for half of yesterday, rats swam past us during the command conference.

'They're gnawing the wire, sir.' Mason my batman was at my elbow. He knows a thing about animals being a veterinary student. Why he isn't in the transport corps is beyond me.

'How do you know, Mason?'

'I've heard the sizzles, sir. They get well and truly fried, especially after this sort of deluge.'

There'd been outages on the phones enough times since the rain started. Sergeant Goss and his men had traced the wires all the way up and down the line and found nothing. I didn't want to hear it was rats, for Private Sligo stopped a bullet trying to sort it out before the last stunt. His body's still out there about a yard from the enemy trenches.

'Evans, are you listening?' Having lost his horse with a broken leg a few hours earlier, the brigadier was in a foul mood.

'A rat, sir. Carrying a tin of bully beef between its teeth.'

He grunted and, pulling his boot off, handed it to his batman. The leather was hard with mud, the socks beneath were the dark of old blood.

'The Tommies are on for a push down south. So the question from above is – can we bleed the Hun divisions there?'

'Bring Fritz up here?' I asked

'We'll get the sixty-pounders going – over 250 howitzers to follow. That should get them worried about this front.'

'That's one decent dose of rations,' I said. A gun every fifteen yards of Hun line. 'Do the Tommies have enough to keep them quiet while we hop over?'

'More than enough. Our orders are to get them moving around – free up the Somme advance before they dig in over at Pozières.'

It was looking like a Tommy show with us making noise, but the boys would have to be told differently.

Times were noted and I duly issued orders to the unit commanders regarding their positions and the time for hopping over.

7

9.30 p.m.

The barrage started at 5.35 and heaven help any of the stragglers who were caught out in no-man's-land. The field phone rang and Lieutenant Simons was onto it.

'The front will be hot for a good five hours yet,' the general said. 'So use your own judgement on the hour for the hop over. Your men are fresh, aren't they?'

'Been in for five hours.'

'Plenty of time for an advance then. The Welsh boys can drive the bayonets in after, eh?'

As he spoke, I could picture the general's sandy complexion at the other end of the line. He's a red-haired giant from Queensland who'd burnt to a crisp in Egypt. His men had been held to account for some bad stuff over the Turks, they say, and I myself had seen the tufts of hair and the shredded uniforms which drifted from the sands on the spot. There's no black man's earth pit to hide your dirty linen in the Sinai.

'It's a bit tight, sir.' I suppose I was hoping to squirm my boys out of it.

'Your relief will finish them off, no doubt. Those Welsh boys are all right.'

Maybe a laugh but it was drowned by an explosion falling short in no-man's-land. There might well be boys out there still alive from the last stunt. Maybe not now.

'Assuming the lines are clear, of course. No point in more casualties before they've even made it into the trenches.'

A clean drop for the Tommies then. The general is a career man. Another one spotting an op to get to Blighty for good among the real blood of the Empire. Why our own Australian blood isn't good enough,

I cannot say, but any man who would ask me in the trenches would be told to get on and dig. Some must get along home when this do is over.

The battalion log was splattered with mud, but no blood so far for the day. Turning to the day, I could see by the light of a spluttering flare – my twenty-fourth birthday, but I didn't bother noting it. No cards from home yet. Rumour that another ship has gone down in the Atlantic with 5,000 tonnes and mail for 100,000 men.

'Target trenches assaulted with bombardment.' I tried to keep my writing tidy because the Tommies note these things and words on carelessness could carry up the chain. 'Trench assault for 6.50. Sections 1 to 4 lead, sections 5 to 8 reserve.'

I thought I was leaving the sap for the last time. Simons had my helmet ready, and had even rubbed a smear of mud from the lip. A corporal was cursing at someone – his newspaper had been stolen, so he was out of sorts. Nerves probably. The poor chap hasn't much to do while the bombardment lasts. He's a tyrant but I try to keep my distance from the enlisted discipline. While I buttoned my coat, some sapper was getting a serving.

'Henderson is a lousy bastard anyway. He didn't use the oil like I said, the lazy cuss. Too much time playing cards.'

'But trench digging needs legs, sir, working legs. See, he can't get the boot off, it was…'

'Lucky bastard has a leg then.' That's for now and the corporal knows it. 'All right, the useless bastard can walk to the ambos. It's only a mile or so.'

The stations are full of the foot rot and they say the smell in the field hospitals is like a glue factory. At this rate, there'll be no men left to hop over.

Our bombardment was over-long. Who the hell didn't follow orders? A sweet bird-filled dawn, and still we poured fire into the Hun lines. And all to bring more of the b—s up from the south onto us. I was glad I'd made a note in the log. A mention in dispatches may come of the stunt if we get anyone through. Dear Lil will be proud of her old brother.

Plunkett, the lieutenant of section 5, watched the units to his left go over and just shook his head. Too good a man for this show. My whistle blew to obliterate the birdsong – it was no time for beauty. I marched the line myself to make sure they'd gone. I'd heard of a Tommy captain who'd gunned a man to make the others hop over. No need with my boys. They were over and in the thick of it while the shells fell in the midst of them – some rabid frenzy had got into them. But the shells – sending wood splinters, flesh and wet earth to the skies. A smeared breeze returned and smacked the reserved men in the face. An hour and still the men kept hopping over as the Hun machine guns strafed our lines. So much for the howitzers keeping them quiet.

No reports for over an hour – so many officers missing. Word came from section 2 – some incursions in the left trenches, a few bayonets released. Hundreds trapped behind the lines. The Huns had swept right back into their trenches after the guns had finished. The binoculars brought strange reports of men crying for their mothers out in no-man's-land. Fritz popping at the wounded crawling in the holes. An observation balloon might see something. If I'm lucky, the pilot will live long enough to make a report.

7.30 p.m.

I've written 'Relief 7 o'clock' in the log, but regret it. The Welsh lads are still a mile back, because the major turned out to be a true Sandhurst boy and followed his orders. Sandy hair like the general, freckles from training on the Wiltshire downs. A perfect pair they'd make, if they ever met.

My men are a carpet in the trenches. It's hard to tell who the dead are, and the fresh wounded keep flopping back into the trenches atop the old, jumbled arms and steaming guts pressed together. The stretcher bearers are nowhere in sight, Sausage Valley too hot for passage. Who can blame the Huns? We overstepped the mark by two hours and 500,000 shells.

The Welsh major stepped over the lads where he could, I'll give him that credit, it's more than my own would do.

'A clean relief was the order.'

'Yes, well as clean as can be.' I was selling him a crippled mule. My men would clog these trenches for hours yet.

I could see the pity in the man's eyes. He stalked amongst the bodies. The stench of burning flesh – a handsome boy's face atop a charred torso. Unlucky lad – mortar had set alight the wicker wall of his cubbyhole.

'There are no duckboards in sight,' he pointed out. 'You've given me no passage, Evans.'

We were in the widest of the trenches, but the ground was a humpy of sandbags and corpses, hard to distinguish. We stood side on while exhausted men slumped against the walls, bayonets spiking the dead flesh which buffered the parapets above.

'How am I to get them in?'

'The ambos are at it. But…'

Truth be said, little was being done during the barrage. The stretcher bearers were probably lighting up a billy. I'd seen it done before, the tea brewing while flies sucked on a body in front of them.

'We'd lose twenty out of a hundred just getting into the place.'

There was no answer to that. I'd have said the same.

'When relief can be achieved, get on the blower, Evans. Well, old fellow, I'll…' He mumbled something, and climbed out of the sap. He'd come on foot, and trotted like the devil through the gully back to the unit.

I'm without relief for hours. My men sit or stand in pillbox doorways as the sky burns. Drizzle and gas make a fog in our miserable valley. My men are reduced to animals. They see to their needs in whatever corner they can. The flesh of dead mates is nothing but a cushion for their heads. Such is our situation.

'Dear Christ!' I hear myself curse.

Simons is staring at me, and my near panic has spooked him. 'Sir?' he asks. 'Sir?'

It's enough to remind me of my duty. 'Get the field hospital,' I say at last.

He's onto the phone. His sweat is on the handpiece which he passes to me.

'Where the hell are the bearers?' I yell.

'Er. Unable to link up, sir.' It's that lazy lance corporal from A Company I've heard so much about. 'No mules available for pulling. It's slow.'

I guess they're bogged down in the shell holes again. 'No excuses. All of them to the sap right now.'

'The gully's clogged, sir.'

'Yes, I'm sure it is. Well, it's bloody got to move. I'll send men to get it cleared.' Where the men will come from I cannot say but it seems to activate the fellow.

Walking wounded straggle past to the entrance to the sap and it's all I can do not to beat them with my stick to get them out of my trenches. They do their best. Before long they're out and hobbling on the duckboards which lead to the gully. It's not enough. The lying wounded are still everywhere. I should call for the red flag but Fritz knows better. We paid no heed to his flag. God knows how many of their wounded were shot to bits in no-man's-land this morning. I've been told a blinded chap's been out there hobbling in circles for twelve hours begging Fritz to finish him off. They're giving it their best shot, but the fellow just won't die.

8

8 p.m.

An unlucky shell has hit a pillbox full of men and what a mess it has made. Dear God, it will set us back a day, I can see relief stretching till the week is out, and by then my men will be nothing but fly feast. Soon there are the moans – my leg, my arm and so on.

The bearers are getting through at last. Here they are, the pairs of hunched men with their collapsed crucifixes between them. They creep around the pillbox, which is a cauldron of wailing. They slow up for some reason.

'Leave them!' I hear myself yell. 'To the sap – now!'

There's no argument from them. One near-death is the same as another. Snail's pace, they take one man away, then another. All too slow. The screaming from the hit pillbox keeps on.

I should be away and let them do it, but I must keep them to the task. The pillbox is a distraction I can't afford. Another set of carriers. The lad at the tail of this stretcher has dropped his end, is standing and watching the ruined pillbox.

'Private!' Move – leave them!' The pillbox wounded are time-wasters, dead and dying flesh, and anyway not in my trenches. 'Private! Move now!'

He's a pale-faced lad. His green eyes fix me in the murk. There's hatred there for a second and I can't say I blame him.

'But this!' He's a brave lad to point it out to me, so maybe he'll survive this stunt.

'There are wounded down here who've been waiting longer. Step lively, man!' I point so there's no confusion in the din.

He's about to talk back, too fresh to know the punishment for disobeying an order. His mate leans back and shoves him in the chest

38

to stir him, and in a minute they're off to it. The pillbox is a steaming mass of angles, greys and browns and a glimmer of drooling pink. A feeble boy is in there crying for help.

Before I get back to the dugout, a shell pummels the parapet in front of me and I huddle amidst the men. One man has a cigarette in his mouth still burning and, realising he's dead, I take the smoke and give it to the shaking lad opposite. Back in section 5, Plunkett is shouting orders at his foul-mouthed best. A fine horseman, he's wasted in the mud. His horse was sold from under him to the Gypos for hack work back in March but, biting his lip, he got on with it.

'The guns are knocked out, so section 1 has been chopped up, I'm afraid.' A grim smile. He's a good man, his first thought always the offensive one, though no man in his right mind would hop over in this shelling. His next words are obliterated in the din.

There's no doubt the Huns have the rations on tap and plenty of reserves. The men around us sink like babies in the womb, just waiting, waiting for the lollipop to drop on them.

A pair of bearers climb over us. I must hold my tongue to keep from barracking as if from the sidelines of the battalion rugby. At this intensity, Fritz will obliterate this mile of line. We were supposed to be softening *them* up. There's slipping in the mud. A wounded man drops from a stretcher into the lap of a crouching infantryman about to relieve himself. The infantry man's knees make a neat shelf and, dropping his privates, he cradles the poor blighter's head. The major is returning at 1 o'clock to see the state of things. I have only a few hours to clear the trenches.

The sky is on fire. It's worse than Gallipoli, this relentless dumping of shells, the thud of bullets hitting bodies, splintered timbers cartwheeling above us, the tremor of collapsing trenches and the endless phut, phut of the guns.

By the time I reach my bunker, Fritz has dropped more gas. My candle flickers and it takes me a while to see that Simons is not standing. His arm is beside him, making a pool on the floor of the bunker. I call out, 'Bearer!' But, of course, no one hears.

The private on guard duty has wrapped up the wound and gone back to his cards. 'Went out to deal with a gas casket, poor sod. I tried for a bearer but…' he said.

I couldn't blame him for that resigned tone. I've often heard it among enlisted men when addressing defective officers. This doesn't hearten me, but in the line there's little time to fret over the opinion of the ranks.

'Do you need morphia, Simons?' My question is for nothing, as the field ambulance is two miles away and no possibility of getting any under the barrage. The bearers will be scuttling about up top, brave b—s, clearing the lines. Simons is at least out of the way.

'Sir?' His answer is a feverish blink. If there is pain, it's buried too deep to be felt.

The ring of the field telephone sends one of the privates shrieking like a hyena. A raw lad from Melbourne Grammar School, he's stuck his fingers in his ears to keep the fury away. A boy in a thunderstorm, what's the use of them? Bawling him out, I have to take the call myself, yelling for a repeat of the message and, slipping on the bloodied floor of the sap, I come down on my knee. A report from section 4: the machine guns have been knocked out, no one knows when, but probably before the hop over.

'How many got through?

The line descends into noise. Shelling on the wire maybe. Hanging up I trudge into the mud. I'm thirsty after thirty-six hours and a ruptured water bottle, but I couldn't eat a biscuit if I had one.

9

11.45 p.m.

The most recent Hun prisoner we've taken has a bit to say about our shelling, and it's a queer patriot who smiles at his own men being shot to ribbons. A university man from Dusseldorf, he has a glass eye which reflects the shellfire in a pearly gleam. He claims to be royal, no doubt a ruse to get special treatment.

'It is very bad in my home now. There is no faith in the victory. Four months at the most and then the end, I am sure.'

He's been well ratted by the three patrolmen who snatched him creeping past our sap. It's alarming that he almost made it through to the railhead, where he intended to strip naked, smear himself with mud and moan as if in shock. It's fortunate we took him, as he might have useful information about the strength of their reinforcements. The patrol could have shot him, and I confess a natural military disdain makes me also inclined to. Sipping cocoa while our mortars pump heat into his own men.

Rubbing his hands together, he raises his head above the shelling. 'I am a medical man, I have no taste for soldiering.' A quiet field hospital behind the lines is what he wants. A hole for his coward's behind.

'You can carry till we are relieved. Then you'll go behind lines.'

He huffs and rifles through his pockets, but there's nothing to make his case with. My men have already ratted him of his silver star. Damn the Hun. They would have their voices shouted across all the nations. A Hun has no natural humility. I have chosen well to give him into the hands of the stretcher bearers. Their hollow hearts would chill the sun.

1 a.m.

A despatch rider brings news of the Tommy end of the stunt, up near the bluff where the pocket of forest was the last time I looked.

1,500 wounded in the first couple of hours, the Hun's shelling fine, so my guess about the reserves wasn't far from the mark. We've taken hits in Willoughby's battalion. Their machine guns were targeted and that's no surprise. Their observation balloons have been over more than once in the last week. They'd have had our guns right enough.

A call came at 12.40 from the railhead – the ammo had been hit and taken a dozen to the sky and back. No chance of more iron rations for hours, us sitting pretty for Fritz to work over. A lively time for the Welsh boys. I hope the push on the Somme was worth all this.

The bearers come in pairs regular now, descending and loading up the wounded, the trenches sticky with mud and the leaking remains of limbs. But the paths are clearing. There won't be many men trickling back in now.

2 a.m.

Relief at last. The major's batman has put a rug down to cover the pool of blood where Simons lost his arm. The major has cigars in his pockets but doesn't offer me one. I can't bother to note again in the log. Leave it for the Welsh boy.

Making my way down the line, a few of my men are still straggling up the ladders while the Tommies are crawling into the fetid hollows of mud. A sergeant is pulling the charred corpse from the cubbyhole so he can set up his bed there. The ingenuity of a man made captive by our circumstances is a thing of wonder. Above, I notice that Plunkett has done well and the bodies are stacked in a neat pile. All good lads. At the entrance to the sap, the stretcher bearers have trudged a boy to pulp. Some poor fatigue man will have to find his pay book in the muck. I hope the grog ration has made it from the railhead, for some sod will need it tonight.

Giles

10

Dear Lionel,

Your newspaper received and all my thanks for sending the *Morning Post*. Perhaps if you cut out the ads and so reduce weight, you can reduce the cost of postage. The boys and I get so much from the stories, such as they are. How do those newsmen get their ideas about the Huns? Here's one – a cartoon with a snivelling Hun, hook-backed with a bayonet through him saying, 'How can we fight against these great strong Australian boys? We are such smaller and weaker creatures, what chance have we?' Whoever drew such stupidity has not carried a Hun across a sodden field. I would be willing to wager that most Huns are over six feet tall. An officer commented on parade that these Huns, being veterans of so much fighting, are the fittest of the lot.

They do look after us all right and no one at home need worry about me. The infantry take the greatest risk. I wouldn't be sheltering in one of those trenches for any money. At least carrying keeps the limbs strong and exercised. The infantrymen shrink like cripples.

Last night, we carried five men whose only trouble is the cursed trench foot. These men are a source of shame to themselves as well as their officers, for there's honour in stopping a Hun bullet, but not in a rotten leg. The hardest carry was the last, but isn't that always the case with any odious job, Lionel? This fellow got my attention by attempting to handle the stretcher as if to help, silly fool.

'I can still do my bit,' he'd said. 'With or without a horse. Right?'

I hadn't recognised him, but there he was. The Light Horse groom, Shilling. The Peninsula man. He was little help, his trembling legs and the real stretcher case heavy enough. Besides, Cockie dislikes talking on the job. Anyway, the groom was hobbling like an old man – he should have had crutches but there were none available for him. Too many men with the rot and not enough supplies.

'I have him,' I said. 'Just keep on while you can.'

We would see how that went, for the mud was not receding.

'Give it me.' He tried to push me aside. 'I won't have a city dandy work while I stand idly by.'

Did he think that, with his weakened leg, he could do better than me and Cockie, who have been carrying wounded for a month now?

I was about to raise my voice at him but then a great crack split the night. It was the steeple of the church which had shattered and then fell. A tremor ran through the earth as the slate tip hit the ground. Then the rumble of exploded shells over at Gordon dump. Fritz had been trying for the dump for five days. We all stopped and listened to the noise. If the railhead was gone, heaven help all those roughly stitched-up men.

'That's near number 3 station,' I said.

'Keep going!' called Cockie. The Light Horse man started limping hard but in a determined machine-like gait. It wouldn't last. I'd seen men do that with a rotten leg and it made cook's work for the doctors.

'Here, rest will you.' I wanted him to stop then, and so urged him to move to a sitting position. He might never ride again. I imagined the tears on his sweetheart's face, his broken father.

'I'm fit enough,' he insisted stubbornly.

'Why are you here, man? You're a groom.'

'My colonel's dead. Nutty's lame, the poor girl.' Choking up over his mare, he refused to let go of the stretcher.

'You're walking wounded.' I shouldered him.

Cockie wouldn't take too much of this. 'Follow the rules, man. You're wounded!'

'Bugger the rules!'

On his last word, the shell hit a ruined wagon on our left. A flash landed on my closed eyes. It was like a punch from a bullying giant. The stretcher wobbled as Cockie and I staggered.

'Blast that mud.' Shilling cursed more than that, but I dare not write it out. 'It's cruel when the earth flies. Damned cruel!'

You see, Lionel, he thought it was just wet earth, and indeed it can spit with cold and shattered stone against the cheeks. But, as fate would have it, there were shell splinters beneath the wagon left there by Fritz when he had this field. Up it came, Lionel, in splinters of black, the pieces slicing at our faces. We felt it like sleet. As I write now, my fingers sting. The metal is in my fingertips gnawing its way in.

Thank God I'm not a surgeon, for their work is hard enough. They work day and night under filthy tallow lamps, topping up their alcohol supplies with rum. More than one drinks as he works, it's said to calm the nerves. I'm thankful to our parents, Lionel, that our family doesn't hold with drinking, for though liquor may be needed in order to saw off a shattered arm, it's nothing but a pestilence upon the men of the army as a rule. In the villages, the general state is one of inebriation, and the officers have little control over men who refuse to parade without a rum ration. The rank is so depleted, Lionel, the best men of the XXXX Battalion have two-thirds been snuffed out with lost eyes, splintered shoulders, blasted chests or guts or private parts, and the never-ending line of men with rotten legs.

And so, down we went into a flooded shell hole, the poor lad from Bendigo on the stretcher groaning as the stretcher hit the water. He started trembling. His face had been hit as well, though maybe his whimpers were from a nightmare. I pray so, for what cruelty can slice a man's face while his guts are split amongst his clothes? Cockie's a strong 'un and, between us, we held the poor chap aloft, but the shelling was tight. The Hun had our mark. It's said they target us bearers, disrupting the train to the ambulances as a means to slowing down the army.

Thus engaged, we lost sight of our walking wounded with the trench foot. He had in fact slipped and the water was at his chest. The fury of the shells so deafening, I wonder I heard his whimper. He was nearly drowned, poor chap, his mouth taking mud and water and pieces of shell. Without thinking, I let the stretcher go. It's only natural to save a man from drowning.

'Oh, blast them to h—' This was me speaking, Lionel, but it

seemed like another speaking through my mouth. Perhaps my ears were stopped with mucus, they seep so when unable to take more of the fury of the shelling. And then this queer me I did not know came forth, and glad I was, for I was strangely comforted by it.

'Fritz has a witch's heart,' I heard myself cry. 'A demon he is, true enough. We'll send him to hell. Straight to hell!'

A queer set of words and laced with fury, my arms dragging aloft from the water the boy with the rotten leg. So there we stayed through it. We couldn't move. I closed my eyes and, while the mud whacked my helmet, I scarcely remembered the other boy on the stretcher. I refused to look, for there was only Cockie to see to him. One is enough under bombardment. For some reason, I knew it was only right to make my choice. Surely it's better to be sure of one man than to try for two and lose both? With every shell, the sky was alight as if fired by God's anger.

Opening my eyes at last, I saw the dim shape of Cockie clutching something to him, a jumble of cloth and mud, his mouth hanging open as he gasped. The man's heart isn't strong. The skin of his cheek was the insipid colour of steamed fish.

When the shelling stopped, it took us some time to notice the quiet. My ears were clogged and it wasn't with mud. Strange that I could hear the boy breathing and also Cockie. So loud they both seemed, men's lungs heaving like bellows in a closed workshop. Noise in the shell hole, dull and thick, comes at you hard.

'Where's the lad?' I called out. 'The boy from Bendigo? Where is he?' I'd lost sight of him, the boy with a mane of thick black hair. The lads called him Darkie. The other strange me started muttering curses and gibberish that even I didn't recognise. He's here to stay, I suspect. Molly will not know me – after all this murder for the King, what good if we cannot enjoy the same companionship we had before the war?

'Oh.' Poor Cockie's lungs had caught gas and laboured heavy. 'Oh, he's gone.'

I saw it then, the bundle of sodden rags was half-buried in the mud, the crook of the elbow rocking like a broken tent.

'Too heavy,' I suggested. What was I to say to him? Two hours holding a man aloft in water is no task for a well man, let alone a sick one.

'No,' answered Cockie. 'He just stopped breathing, so I let him go.'

So, Lionel, I had chosen my man wisely. The Light Horse lad had taken the shelling badly. He was clinging to my chest as if to snuggle back into his mother's womb. It took some minutes to calm him and even as I said over and over, 'There, there,' I wondered when the next shell would fall.

The world was too quiet to be true after the bombardment. In many ways, Lionel, it's better to remain under fire in this scrape. When one has time to stop and think of the mess and the unnaturalness of it all, that's when the mind starts upon it, turning it over and letting it all sink into oneself, as polluting as this strange grey stuff which is now in my fingertips.

11

Dragging Shilling from the shell hole, we got him upon the stretcher, which was then free. He made a dreadful weight upon it but at least there was just one of him. We had him under our care now and not a nuisance beside us on the track. His face was a circle of mud and I feared his eye was ruined with a splinter of shell casing. What miracle had spared me and Cockie I do not know. God has a purpose we cannot fathom in this hellish battle and I feel it was He who has filled me with a new courage.

As we started off, heat rose from the earth, the spilt damp earth, and such rich soil. The worms are lush upon every piece of meat, animal and human, which stays upon it. We were not close to the station. No, a good mile on it was, but Cockie stopped and spoke through the dark.

'I'm lost.'

I looked for the steeple, and if it had been there I'd have seen it by the flash of the ammo up north. All I saw was tree stumps, a line of men bobbing on the horizon of torn earth, and then darkness. We slumped to the mud.

Cockie's not well, he should be back in Blighty, but his temper puts him out with the sergeant. He's forty-five years old and shouldn't have come.

Three of us waiting, lying in the mud. The stretcher case trembled. The lad was going mad on it. Somewhere close was the stink of old graves.

'What shall we do?' I asked.

Distant shells. Thank God our section of the line had gone quiet. More work ahead then. The call would go up everywhere for the next twenty-four hours, 'Bearers!' Oh, I'm learning to hate the word!

Cockie was up and somehow we got moving again, left and right along the twisting muddy tracks, hoping it was south, watching the horizon for a landmark of some sort. To the right was coughing and the mewing of men weakening at their ends. Words in German, the sharp explosion of a pistol fired in the dark. But I'm too used to that sound now, Lionel. It brings me only relief knowing there will be one less to carry.

We were another two hours at it – the mud sucking us down at one point so I felt the earth rise like walls, all peppered with stones, rotting wood and splintered bones. All the time Cockie panting and, if it hadn't been for the carry upon the stretcher, I suspect we would have just collapsed there in the filth as others had before us. We hadn't eaten since 5.30 a.m. the day before – bread and butter, a teaspoon of dried milk, tea. A day's ration of water doesn't last long.

It was only when we met the party coming in the opposite direction that we knew we were heading too far to the north. Mounted Englishmen, a major and his batman, and I felt for the poor beasts upon the track. Too many mules have gone under in the quagmire and been left for dead. It took them some time to see us but a flare lit the sky and we came into their view.

'Gawd, what a sight you are!' the startled major said and the batman peered down into us as if we were zoo specimens.

We must have been a fright to see with our faces mud gashed and splintered with tin.

'Hurry round, Dawson, before the horse takes fright.'

The man's noise set Shilling awake and in fright he tried to flee the stretcher. Grabbing him, I felt nothing but the wetness of his leg. They'd have a dreadful time getting the shoe off him.

'A Hun! There, a Hun!'

There wasn't a Hun within a mile of us, unless he counted them in the bodies around us.

The Englishmen led their horses to the high ground away from us. The batman called back something about duckboards. Thus I knew we were close to the path again.

This time it was Cockie holding us up. 'I can't, lad. See – my hands.'

He'd lost his gloves whilst inebriated in the village and the sergeant was making him wait for another pair. A mean man, the sergeant, who thinks to buy favour with the captain through the over-use of discipline.

'See the state of them. They're making it awful hard, lad.'

Truth be told, I couldn't see too well in the dark, though dawn was creeping on the horizon. Mud and blood make a gritty slough and I guessed that was the trouble. Cockie's weakness took me by surprise, Lionel. Unfit men make war a burden beyond endurance.

'Cockie, get up.' I slapped his poor old balding head. 'Get going. The duckboards are only half a mile away.'

So the Englishman said, and I couldn't blame Cockie for sighing deeply as he rose and glued his rank hands to the stretcher. They say he joined to be with his son and the boy is dead now. When the carry started moaning, I pushed harder from my end, Cockie stumbling, but I would not let them rest. The carry shuddered and groaned in a delirium. Half a mile, I started to count again. Dawn was somewhere and the birds started. One flitted low across the mud en route to a lone tree over across the lines.

We met duckboards at last, the Englishmen had been right, and in the dawn I recognised a ruined tree where I'd left a man one day a few weeks past. You may wonder how I knew it, Lionel, in a land without features of any kind. Well, in these bewildering heaps of mud, a mound of new grass denotes a corpse beneath. There he was, the chap a positive floral exhibition. Reaching out, I pulled at a few flowers which had sprouted from his innards, shoving them amongst my clothes. There's so little of joy in this war, we grasp at it wherever we find it.

We were close to the station then and I called out to Cockie, 'Not far, Cockie. Half an hour carry, if that!'

The carry rose from a delirium and reached a hand towards me. 'Nursie!'

I had stopped listening to his grizzling. He was unrecognisable from the horseman I had briefly known, the Peninsula veteran with the easy word. Perhaps I was harsh as I slapped away his hand.

It took us a good hour to reach the station, which is nothing but a tent amidst a pile of empty chloroform bottles. The entrance was obscured by the steam of a laundry tub. Fritz could be heard pouring heat into the trenches again somewhere north. The wounded mind can play odd tricks and so it seemed with the Light Horse man as he waited on the stretcher to be seen.

'Hey, it's Nursie! Little Nursie, here!'

Some strange name conjured from his delirium. As far as I knew, he thought of another and not a man who'd carried him for miles through the gully. His hand rose as if to drag at my coat. Instinctively, I pulled back and tucked the hand into his chest. For it's enough to bear their bodies without also bearing their torment.

12

One of the other bearers had a billy going. There are some advantages to this job and access to a primus stove is one of them. A Hun doctor was stepping among the bodies, sniffing for signs of death. The stench of foot rot was everywhere, so how such a method would provide clues of mortality I cannot say. There are rumours that they've burnt bodies down for fuel over in Bapaume but I don't believe it.

The Light Horse man was still going on and what a noise the wounded can make with so little air in their lungs.

'You brought this man?' the Hun asked, peering down at Shilling.

I answered him yes. The tea tasted of metal and I wondered if shell powder had leached into the water.

'The boot is still on.' He was a stern barking man. His Hun uniform told me he was an officer, but he had no ribbons left on him. 'You did not think to remove? So many miles with him, and you did not... See the difficulty? What this fellow will have to endure, and with the boot?'

It's so like the doctors to find fault with us. I exchanged glances with the AMC corporal next to me and together we held our peace and took our tea. Only five hours of rest and then another twenty-four hours of carry ahead.

'Ah go, go!' the Hun yelled.

I could see no Australian or English doctor at the station, and it's a fine war when we leave our wounded to the enemy, even behind the lines.

The boy wailed as they took his leg off, so no doubt they were short of morphia, or perhaps the proud German was exacting Hun justice upon us.

The YMCA tent in this section is a fine one with a wooden floor, a large urn, cheese sandwiches and tinned fruit. Searching out Cockie there, I found he had decamped to a hut with the other AMC boys and was playing cards. He had colour in his face again, and I offered him some tea, but he was already warmed by liquor.

'The carry's likely dead by now,' I said, and so it turned out to be.

'A waste of a carry,' he said, his mouth glistening wet in the dimness of the pillbox. 'That boot was fixed on, no doubt.'

There are piles of boots in the gully behind the station, Lionel, and some still have legs in them. The army is yet to understand the need for salvage bags and the hygiene of modern standards. I must ask the Hun doctor how his people cope with the mess but, from his temper, I fear I know his answer. After all, Lionel, the Hun, for all his cleverness, was no more prepared for this adventure than we.

In all my scribbles, I have not asked after Mother, so please send me all the news, and any clippings on local events is welcome. The land prices you mention continue to astound me, and I'll be curious when I finally obtain leave to Blighty to see how their prices compare. I suspect it's an unfair comparison, as New South Wales still has uncleared land aplenty, whereas population is a tighter fit in the home of Empire. I'm not in a hurry for promotion, so please don't ask again. From what I see, it brings more difficulty than it's worth and I would miss my pals in the AMC. In this scrape, one needs good company more than a few bob.

I must finish my letter now. Australian mail leaves in half an hour and I'll miss it again if not careful.

PS: I don't like the letters from Molly, and there I was thinking I'd put her nicely in the path of English officers, by urging her to take the move to London. I cannot make out the confusing officialdom we must go through to write to each other – it's worse than when she was in the hospital in France and only thirty miles from the front. Her last note came in an aerogram stamped 'Passed by the Censor' and with an officer's scrawl across the back. It gives some Tommy a neat job, no doubt. Again, the less said the better, with Mr Censor listening in!

Your brother, Giles

*

Dear Molly,

I have too much to say to you and cannot find the words upon which to continue the account of my war. I'm still carrying in XXX section, and don't mind saying that it's a hellish job. I didn't know there were so many guns in the world before I came to France.

Heaven knows if you'll get this letter – the Australian Army post is better than most, but what functions well amidst the chaos of the front? Yes, Molly, I've been in the thick of it and am by now an old hand in the AMC. Exhaustion makes it difficult to write by these spluttering candles. Perhaps it will excuse me in some way for whatever I've done to miff you.

The censor will destroy this letter if I tell you of my movements and the progress of the AMC on this front, so I'll say nothing. But what else to say, old Mol? For, as you know from the hospital, the war fills one's entire mind and needs to be got rid of some how. Otherwise madness follows. There's no one else, Mol, not old Lionel who is a stick but, being eight years older than us and rightly caring for Mother, cannot truly feel the emotions of this war as we can. I cannot be angry with you for your curt notes, for no doubt the Tommy hospitals are getting you down. But cheer up, Mol, it's not forever, and when leave comes, I'll be over and with you in a flash and, boy, what a time we'll have touring the sights!

I've just written to Lionel, but what can I tell them which isn't polished and somehow softened? You've seen the men, Mol, you've dressed those horrid shattered bodies. I would have everyone at home proud of our work for the Empire.

Enclosed is a flower which I picked from a field nearby and secreted in my pay book. You see it has been pressed well. Looking at it, I sometimes fear I won't see you again, for war can do anything to people. Your letters are proof enough that this war has bitten you hard. It grieves me that we cannot talk as we used to, feet up at the fire after my day at Ingroves and you still mastering that complicated sock pattern the army issued. When we meet next, you might be engaged (no, don't laugh!) and I might have been decorated – even dentists get medals in this scrape, it's a real joke. Don't you agree? Please write and tell me if so – with your own words, not that Tommy form stuff. I miss your old laughing self – has it gone with the war? What will you make of me, and my new ways?

Even the gaps between Mother's letters stretch and stretch. The days are so full of tiredness, and I'm sure you know what horrors fill my sleeplessness.

No, I'll keep this pressed blossom now. It will await my leave to Blighty – I daren't trust it to this post. Those Tommy officials seem determined to stop us communicating. Only face to face can we really be ourselves again, Mol. I keep your face in front of me during the midnight carries. We have only the English Channel and a couple of train journeys separating us. But you seem further away than ever. Until I hear from you again, old girl.

Your twin brother, Giles

Sidney

13

Private diary of Captain Sidney XXXX Xth Division, AIF, Western Front

Albert 9.30 p.m.

It's odd what men will say to their parents and brothers at home which would be laughed at in the mess hall. I passed one of the veterans today, a man who ran fatigues at the dysentery rest camp on Lemnos. A milder chap you could not meet, but by his letters you would think he'd beaten Abdul single-handed. Bloody and vengeful are his outpourings and how he hopes his dear Ma will benefit from this false account of his, I don't know.

He's running the incinerator in town here. While his papers and ruined boots burn, he reads the *Bulletin* and Henry Lawson. While his deceit is not to be admired, I could not bring myself to censor his fantasies. I have thirty letters to read tonight and, while it's an irksome task, it must be done.

The YMCA writing paper used by many is excellent, captured Hun paper better. Some have been sent paper from home, others use scraps from regimental diaries, while others use the pilfered shopkeepers accounts from the villages. Many have made note of foreign words and figures, many can draw well enough for the newspapers. Some can barely write a line, others could fill a library. Many number the letters and, no doubt, will receive a tally from the folk upon their return of how the army has short-changed them.

Madame brought me onion soup and corn bread for supper, and rattled on about milk and flour shortages. She spoke much and in fast French which I could not understand, but still I listened to her frenzied ramblings. I sleep in her brother's bed. Her husband is a POW near Lübeck, her barn and two dairy cows have been burnt down by a carelessly extinguished propane stove fire of my men's doing. Listening to her is the least I can do. The smoke from the barn is within this very room as I write. The Hun gas pellets haven't made it this far, but some of the fields beyond the village have seen them. Such wasted supply, for barely a man or woman sets foot in the mucked-up dirt now.

The last letter I censored was a joy to read. A corporal telling his sweetheart he was going on leave to Blighty and asking her to come from Liverpool to meet him. If only all letters could be such. I'm reminded of today's decorations in the roofless old church. The statue of the Virgin is still standing up there in the roof, and men say if it falls it will mean our war's end.

No one enjoys these occasions and especially not the Medical Corps men, who believe doctors are overly decorated and so resent the first five men in the parade. I had made a point of recommending Giles XXXXXX for the Military Medal, for surviving Sausage Gully is more than enough proof of bravery. Only an hour before and the sergeant quietly took me aside to give me word of him, and between us we sorted out what was to happen to his medal. A bit of an awkward one so late in the day. It's too late to withdraw the decoration, and why the hell should I? The chap carried under fire, he has served his King, and who am I to say war nerves must manifest in any particular way? And now his letter to his sister is before me, and a damn nuisance it is, for I can't very well send it on to the deceased. The Tommies have much to answer for – I would have spoken to the lad myself, it's my job. Those aerograms can be cruel notes and if a man's mind is stressed, is it any wonder nothing of fact will sink in? It appears her digs took a direct hit from a Zeppelin, worst luck. Ten brave girls blown to bits. Despite official notification, he wrote a further three letters to her.

The sergeant and I had held back the last two returns – no use the boy falling apart and being deemed another of those 'unfit for further service' after the Fromelles fiasco. If his last letters to a corpse aren't evidence of madness, what is? But he could apparently hold his own in the football competition, he continued to carry to the end, and if that is madness, then it's what we want in this war.

It's a miracle he lasted this long, really, deranged by the business but able to the keep the writing up. I could send it to his mother. But what mother would want such panic-ridden scratchings? He was due to be off to Pozières tomorrow along with the rest of advance, Fritz getting a walloping thanks to the 5,000 boys left to rot at Fromelles.

Madame has collected my plates and I can feel the shelling in the bricks behind me. The XXXX Battalion are warming up Fritz for the big push. I have one more letter to censor and I only hope this regimental pen holds out. So much of this war is slashing, cutting, my pen has seen more action than my pistol. So much of the stuff I have deleted is still within me, the cowardly bitterness of men, the numbers, the names of towns and generals and the passage of dates. But before I finish slashing, I'll write to this lad's mother.

*

Dear Mrs XXXXXX,

I write regarding your son Giles. While I was his commanding officer, I was not there when he met with the unfortunate firearms accident. He was a fine young man and his death is a loss to all of us.

*

I've done this task enough times and it's no better than censoring. There are a few additional words about his carrying, his old friend Cockie, his affection for his family, although I have no knowledge of his thoughts, except his last deluded ones. The news of his Military Medal I leave to the end and then I'm done with it. In another time, in another war, there would be time for more words. The right ones of course, for what mother would want details of this sort of end? He'd never been good with pistols and it took him two days to die.

Finishing my letter, I'm aching for my bed. My pen holds out long enough to scrawl some consoling words about the lad having had a good war. It's not for me to argue the point. Tomorrow, Pozières and the next front. After the last debacle, the howitzers will burn the sky above Fritz.

I've censored the last of the letters. I've already decided on destroying the awkward notes from this Giles lad, the stretcher bearer. By tomorrow he'll no longer be my burden.

The pillow under me smells of someone else's cigarettes. Maybe Madame's husband, maybe some Tommy major. Thankfully, I'll never know who that man was.